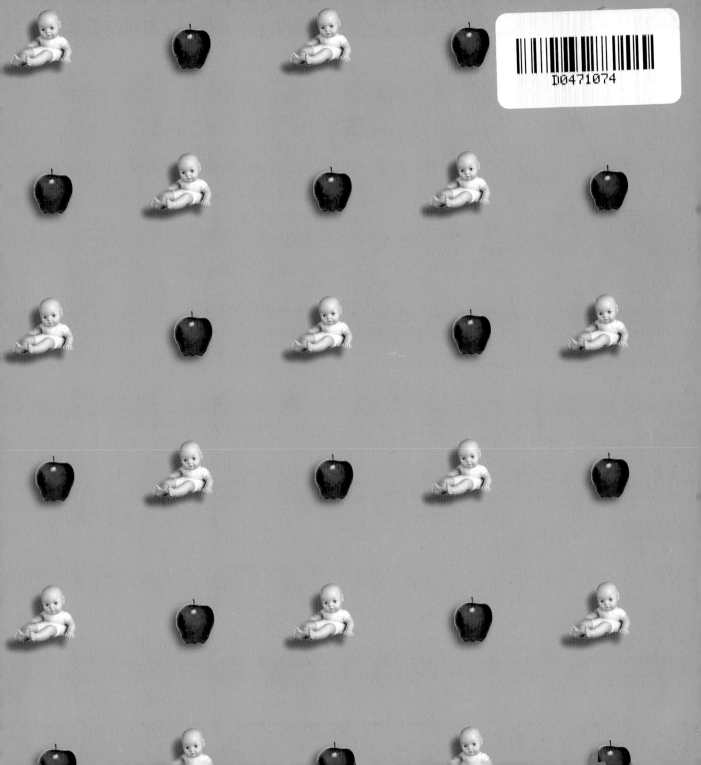

Look What I See!
Where Can I Be?

With My
Animal Friends

by Dia L. Michels

Photographs by
Michael J.N. Bowles

Platypus Media, LLC
Washington, DC
2002

For Cathy Pfeiffer,
whose love of books inspired
generations of children

Enjoy these other *Look What I See!* books by Dia L. Michels
In the Neighborhood
At Home
In China
At the Synagogue
Activity Guide available at PlatypusMedia.com

Library of Congress Cataloging-in-Publication Data

Michels, Dia L.
　　With my animal friends / by Dia L. Michels ; photographs by Michael J.N. Bowles.
　　　　p. cm. — (Look what I see! Where can I be? ; 3)
　　Summary: Photographs depict how, after each day's nap, a baby girl wakes up to a
　　new view of animals at the various places her family visits, and the reader is invited to
　　guess where they are.
　　　　ISBN 1-930775-07-5 (alk. paper)
　　　　　[1. Babies—Fiction. 2. Animals—Fiction. 3. Family life—Fiction.] I. Bowles, Michael
J.N., ill. II. Title.
PZ7.M5817 Wi 2002
[E]—dc21　　　　　　　　　　　　　　　　　　　　　　　　　2002016980

Platypus Media, LLC
627 A Street, NE
Washington, DC 20002
PlatypusMedia.com

1 2 3 4 5 6 7 8 9

Platypus Media is committed to the promotion and protection of breastfeeding.
We donate six percent of our profits to breastfeeding organizations.

Series editor: Ellen E.M. Roberts, Where Books Begin, New York, NY
Project management: Maureen Graney, Blackberry Press, Washington, DC
Book design: Douglas Wink, Inkway Graphics, Santa Fe, NM
Production consultant: Kathy Rosenbloom, New York, NY
Additional photography: Carol Bruce Photography, Arlington, VA

Special thanks to the staff of the following facilities for their help with this
book: Frying Pan Park, Fairfax, VA: horseshoe and goat-milking scenes. Leesburg
Animal Park, Leesburg, VA: petting zoo scene. Carrie Murray Outdoor Education
Campus, Baltimore, MD: iguana scene. National Aquarium, Baltimore, MD: dol-
phin scene. Washington Animal Rescue League, Washington, DC: dog scene.

The author would like to thank the Miller Vizas family and the Deutsch family for sharing their homes with us.
She would also like to thank the National Zoo (Washington, DC) and Brookside Gardens (Wheaton, MD)
for their assistance with the butterfly scene.

Manufactured in the United States of America.

I am going to see
my animal friends
with my family.

On Monday,
I fell asleep
in my wagon.

When I woke up,
I saw a horseshoe.

Where was I?

In the barn.

On Tuesday,
I fell asleep
in my front carrier.

When I woke up,
I saw a bright eye.

Where was I?

At the
petting zoo.

On Wednesday,
I fell asleep
in a wheelbarrow.

When I woke up,
I saw a handful of hay.

Where was I?

At a farm.

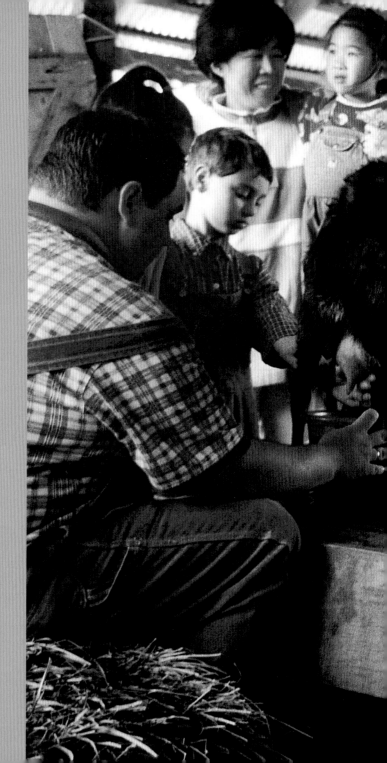

On Thursday,
I fell asleep in my
cloth carrier.

When I woke up,
I saw a bobbing head.

Where was I?

At a wildlife
center.

On Friday,
I fell asleep
in my sling.

When I woke up,
I saw a wet smile.

Where was I?

At the
aquarium.

On Saturday,
I fell asleep in
my basket.

When I woke up,
I saw a friendly face.

Where was I?

At the animal shelter.

On Sunday,
I fell asleep
in my sister's lap.

When I woke up,
I saw orange wings.

Where was I?

Safe and warm
in my sister's
arms.

I am back home again
with a new member
of my family.